GROW YOUR MIND

DON'T PANIC

Written by Alice Harman

Illustrated by David Broadbent

FRANKLIN WATTS
LONDON•SYDNEY

Franklin Watts
First published in Great Britain in 2020 by The Watts Publishing Group
Copyright © The Watts Publishing Group, 2020

Produced for Franklin Watts by
White-Thomson Publishing Ltd
www.wtpub.co.uk

ISBN (HB): 978 1 4451 6927 9
ISBN (PB): 978 1 4451 6928 6
10 9 8 7 6 5 4 3 2 1

Alice Harman has asserted her right to be identified as the author of this Work in accordance with the Copyright, Designs and Patents Act 1988.

Series Designer: David Broadbent
All illustrations by: David Broadbent

Every attempt has been made to clear copyright. Should there be any inadvertent omission please apply to the publisher for rectification.

Printed in China

Franklin Watts
An imprint of
Hachette Children's Group
Part of The Watts Publishing Group
Carmelite House
50 Victoria Embankment
London EC4Y 0DZ

An Hachette UK Company
www.hachette.co.uk
www.franklinwatts.co.uk

MIX
Paper from
responsible sources
FSC
www.fsc.org
FSC® C104740

Facts, figures and dates were correct when going to press.

A trusted adult is a person (over 18 years old) in a child's life who makes them feel safe, comfortable and supported. It might be a parent, teacher, family friend, care worker or another adult.

CONTENTS

A calm mindset

Don't panic! It's easy to say, but it can be pretty tricky to stay calm sometimes, can't it?

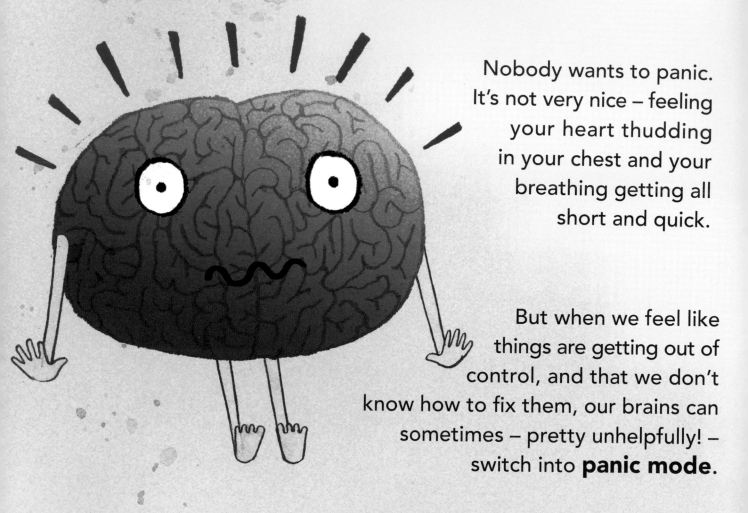

Nobody wants to panic. It's not very nice – feeling your heart thudding in your chest and your breathing getting all short and quick.

But when we feel like things are getting out of control, and that we don't know how to fix them, our brains can sometimes – pretty unhelpfully! – switch into **panic mode**.

So what can we do to avoid panicking? It's not possible to never feel any stress at all, but there are all sorts of things we can do to stop our worries turning into **full-blown panic**.

You can help teach your brain to respond differently to stress, and to react more calmly and positively when problems and difficult situations do pop up in your life.

Sometimes we don't realise how much power we have to **change our brains**, because people often talk about them as if they're fixed – that someone is 'smart', or 'relaxed' or 'a worrier'.

But, in fact, your brain is always changing and growing. You have billions of neurons in your brain that pass messages to one another, and your thoughts and actions can help build new neuron-connecting paths, as well as strengthening helpful ones that already exist.

This also means that if you feel like you can't do something, there's **no need to panic**. You can practise thinking and acting in ways that, over time, can help turn that 'can't' into a 'can'!

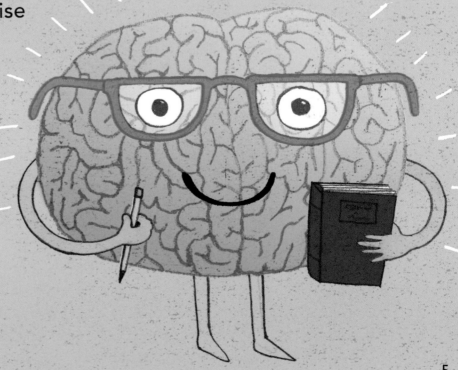

Future friend

One of the best ways to avoid getting stressed and panicking is by being a friend to your **future self**.
But what exactly does that mean?

Well, here's an example – imagine you are given homework on Friday that you have to hand in on Monday, and you know you'll probably feel stressed and panicky on Sunday evening if you try to do it all in a hurry then. What could you do ahead of time to **avoid that panic**?

If your answer is something like, 'Start doing my homework on Friday or Saturday, and split it into chunks so I don't overload my brain trying to get it all done at once', then you already have a pretty good idea of how to be a **future friend** to yourself!

It's all about understanding what might make you feel panicked in the future, and doing what you can now to take away some of that pressure or fear.

Think of three situations that might make you feel panicked, or that have made you feel that way in the past.

Here are some examples, but think of ones that really stand out for you ...

★ **Performing on stage in a school play**

★ **Not knowing what work you're supposed to be doing for a group project that's due in tomorrow**

★ **Having to talk to kids you don't know at a new after-school or weekend activity club**

What can you do ahead of time to be a **future friend** to yourself and make yourself feel more prepared and confident? Try working with an adult to make a mind map of ideas for each situation, then circle the ideas that you think might be most helpful and give them a go!

Nervous or excited?

Do you ever have a fluttery **'butterflies in your stomach'** feeling when you're really excited about something? Perhaps you have a pounding heartbeat in your chest? Maybe you get all fidgety, too, and find it hard to settle down to anything?

If you think about it, it's probably pretty similar to how you feel when you're nervous – right? That's because in both cases your body is releasing a substance called adrenaline, which peps you up to help you tackle whatever you're nervous or excited about.

We often think of being nervous as a bad thing, but it can be a sign that something is important to you and you want it to go well. Instead of thinking, 'Oh no, **I'm really nervous** about this', you could say to yourself, 'Oh wow, **I'm really excited** about this!'

The more you practise thinking positively like this, the easier it gets for your brain to do it. So let's get practising ...

1. Write down what's making you feel nervous. Around it, write or draw what you're worried might happen.

2. Cross through each worry, replacing it with something that you're excited about that might happen. Then add some actions you could take to help make this positive outcome a reality.

For example, if you're starting at a new school you might be nervous about not making new friends. **A more positive take?** You're excited about the opportunity to make new friends, and you're going to join an after-school club to meet people with similar interests.

3. Practise saying to yourself, 'I'm excited about ...' and I'm going to ...', adding in your positive outcome and actions.

Trust yourself

In order for our brains to **grow and change**, we have to challenge them – so if you're finding something difficult, that's a good thing! It's a really great opportunity to boost your brain, and show yourself how putting in effort can help you do things that once seemed near-impossible.

But sometimes we can **feel scared** of trying things that we think are too difficult. We might panic at the thought of even trying, because we don't trust ourselves enough to believe we can succeed.

It's important to remember that just because you can't do something right now, it doesn't mean you'll never be able to. Were you born knowing how to **talk, read or write? No!** But you learned and tried and practised over and over, and you got there in the end.

If you're feeling a bit panicked about a new challenge, it can help to bring to mind a list of past successes. Those might be times when you've changed a habit, learned something new or taken on a responsibility.

Write a list with all the examples you can think of. Think about big steps throughout your life – learning to feed yourself, **get dressed**, read, write and so on.

Keep the list and look at it whenever you worry that you can't do something. The list shows that, with effort and practice, **you can make huge changes**.

Not a competition

Have you ever **fallen behind** a group, maybe because you stopped to tie your shoelaces, and then been shocked to see how far ahead they suddenly were?

You might also get this **panicky feeling** if it seems like you're falling behind others in your class or activity club. Or maybe you want to be the best, but feel like people are catching up to you.

Seeing people in a fixed order, with winners at the top and losers at the bottom, just isn't realistic or helpful. Worrying about our position in this order can make us feel competitive with everyone, and avoid challenges in case we **'fail'**.

In reality, everyone's brain is always changing, so there is no fixed order – and some of the best ways to grow your brain are to take on new challenges and learn from others!

Jana

I always loved playing tennis at my local club, and I was the **best player** for my age. I guess I got used to being the 'star'!

But last year I noticed that one girl, Alexis, was getting way better. I used to be able to beat her without really trying, but I started winning by fewer and fewer points. Then, one day, **she beat me** in a match.

I panicked that maybe I wasn't good after all, and behaved really badly. I told people that Alexis had cheated, and then pretended to be ill to get out of playing the next week.

Then I talked to my dad and he helped me see how it was a good thing that Alexis was challenging me – that I could learn from her and improve my own game. I said sorry to Alexis, and we have so much fun playing together now – we're both **helping each other** to improve loads, too!

Panic button

Have you noticed that when you're panicking, it feels a bit like an **alarm has gone off** in your head? Just like when a real alarm goes off, it can be so shocking that it's hard to think clearly at first – your head feels full of noise, confusion and worry. You might even feel sick, or as though you can't breathe.

So what's going on when you feel this way? Well, your brain is very good at protecting you, but it can also overreact when it thinks you're in danger.

Your **amygdala** is a part of your brain that can react quickly to the world around you and work with other parts of the brain to decide if you're in danger. If the answer is 'yes', your brain hits the panic button!

If you need to escape a charging elephant, it's quite helpful for your brain to shout **'Run! Quick! Now!'** until you do it. It's not so helpful when the 'danger' you're worried about is something like reading out loud in class …

You know how you do fire alarm practices at school, so you know what to do in case of an emergency? Try practising these ways to help your brain when it's **hitting the panic button** but you aren't actually in danger.

1. Take ten deep, slow breaths – imagine your belly inflating like a balloon as you breathe in, and then gently deflating again as you breathe out.

2. Close your eyes and think of a place, a person or pet and an activity that makes you feel happy and relaxed. Try putting them all together – so you might picture yourself singing on a beach with your cat!

3. Scrunch up your fingers and toes really tight, and then let them relax – first one hand, then the other, then your feet one by one. Or you could hunch up your shoulders, then imagine them melting down your back like ice cream.

Remember to always let a trusted adult know if you feel panicky, sick or like you can't breathe. You don't have to deal with these feelings alone.

Reach out

Although we can try lots of different things to help us handle our worries, sometimes we also need to **reach out** and let other people help us.

Everyone feels worried and panicky sometimes, and we all know how difficult and horrible it can be. Sometimes, just telling someone about it can make us **feel better** and less alone.

Even if the trusted adults in your life seem busy and stressed themselves, that doesn't mean they don't care about your problems. They just might not have noticed how difficult you're finding things. Whatever they tell you, **adults can't read minds!**

Ask a trusted adult about starting up regular **'Talk Time'** sessions, where you can take a few minutes to talk over anything that is worrying you.

It's best if these sessions are at a regular time, so no one forgets or ends up not having time to fit it in.

If you find it hard to remember things that worried or bothered you during the day, try keeping a small notebook and **writing them down**, then taking out that notebook for **Talk Time.**

Keep a **Talk Time** diary of what you talk about during the sessions and any plans you make for trying to help you with your worries. This means you can track how you're feeling and how the plans are working out for you.

Everything changes

Change is part of life. The sun rises every day, but apart from that not very much stays the same for ever. Change can be really difficult and sometimes feel quite scary – especially if it's a big change, like moving house or school.

It can make us panic about what will happen, and wish that everything could just stay the same. But we **can't avoid change**, so we have to work on how we react to it instead.

Luckily, our brains are always changing, too – just like every part of our bodies, and everything else in nature. With some time and effort, we can help guide that change so that we end up feeling **calmer and more positive** about new and different situations.

Rodrigo

We moved to a new country last year, and suddenly everything was different and strange. I had to go to a new school and learn a new language, and it was all really **difficult and scary.**

I just wanted to go back home, and for everything to go back to how it was before. I missed my friends so much, and my aunt and cousins who lived just down the street. I felt like I'd never make friends here or do well at school, and it made me feel really upset and panicky.

I talked to my parents about it, and they completely understood. Moving was a big change for them, too! They explained how they tried to **focus on the positives** and new opportunities here, and to take things step by step.

It was hard but I started trying to do the same, and keeping a diary of all the new things I was learning and doing. I'm much happier now, and I've made some really nice friends! I still miss home sometimes but I can now also see the **good things** about coming here.

DO YOUR RESEARCH

If you're feeling **scared or stressed** about doing something new, do some research to get more familiar with it first. It can help you feel more confident about taking on a new challenge.

For example, if you're starting **swimming lessons**, you could ask a trusted adult to help you find videos online that show you what to expect when learning to swim. You could also talk to friends who like swimming and ask them about it.

Maybe you're worried that you don't understand a new subject you've started at school? Ask a trusted adult to help you look for fun books, videos and TV shows so you can get extra information while enjoying yourself – that's the best way to learn!

Charlie

When my mum said we were going on a **camping holiday**, I felt really panicky about it. The only thing I knew about camping was that it meant sleeping in a tent, outside in the dark – and I sometimes feel scared of the dark in my own bed – so I hated that idea!

But when I complained to my friend Aisha at school, she said that she **loved camping**. She went with her family every year, and they did really fun things like toasting marshmallows over a fire and singing songs.

My big sister had been away camping with a club, too, and she showed me photos and videos from her trip – it did look **kind of fun!** She said a girl on the trip had brought a battery-powered night light, and I could ask our parents to get me one.

I felt better about going on the trip then, and even got a bit excited. In the end, I actually had a **really good time** camping – even though it rained a lot!

WHAT CAN I DO?

Sometimes you might worry about lots of things at the same time, so it feels like there's an impossibly **big, dark storm cloud** of worries hanging over you. It's not a nice feeling, and it can make you panic because you don't know how to get rid of it.

Start by trying to pick out the different worries and talking with a trusted adult about how you could feel better about each one.

Some of your worries might be easier to deal with than others. For example, if you're worried about falling behind in class, you can talk to your teacher and parents and get some **extra help**.

But if you're worried about big things, such as climate change, you just can't solve that all by yourself.

It may make you feel a bit panicky to think about things in life that you can't control, but you can help your brain grow and change so it feels more **comfortable** with this idea.

Over time, you can learn to focus on what you can do to help – and to **accept** that there are some things you can't do anything to change.

With the help of a trusted adult, make a mind map of your worries and what you can do to help make each one better. For bigger issues, such as climate change, think about how you can join with others to make a difference. Maybe you could write letters to people in power, or **raise money** for a charity?

For worries that you can't control, such as something bad happening to someone you love, talk about **how that makes you feel** – and how the adults in your life could help you deal with these feelings.

what could go wrong?

When we are really worried about something, we can sometimes **panic** and imagine that the worst possible outcome will definitely happen.

For example, if you're nervous about singing in a school show, you might convince yourself that you'll forget all the words and fall off the stage.

Your brain is trying to help you out by preparing you for the worst, but by making you more nervous it isn't actually being very helpful!

By training your brain to focus on what is **more likely to happen**, and thinking about what actions you can take to make a positive outcome more likely, you can help yourself feel much more confident and calm about new challenges.

Best outcome

Worst outcome

1. Think about something that you're **worried about** going wrong, and the best and worst ways it could possibly turn out. (But keep it realistic – no unicorns flying down to carry you away!)

2. Draw a scale with the best and worst outcomes at either end, and talk with a trusted adult to fill in some 'in-between' outcomes that are quite good, okay or quite bad.

3. Decide together what you think is most likely to happen. Where on the scale is that? Talk about the actions you could take to push the most likely outcome further towards the 'best' end, and think about putting them into an action plan.

IF IT DOES GO 'WRONG'

The reality is that sometimes things don't go quite as well as you might have hoped. It's a part of life and it happens to everyone. And actually, it can be much **better for your brain** than things turning out perfectly!

Scientific studies have shown that people learn more from **making mistakes** than from getting things right. When you make a mistake, special electrical signals spark in your brain and this appears to be linked to better learning over time.

Instead of panicking about making mistakes, think of them as brilliant opportunities to grow your brain. It's time to **get excited** about making mistakes!

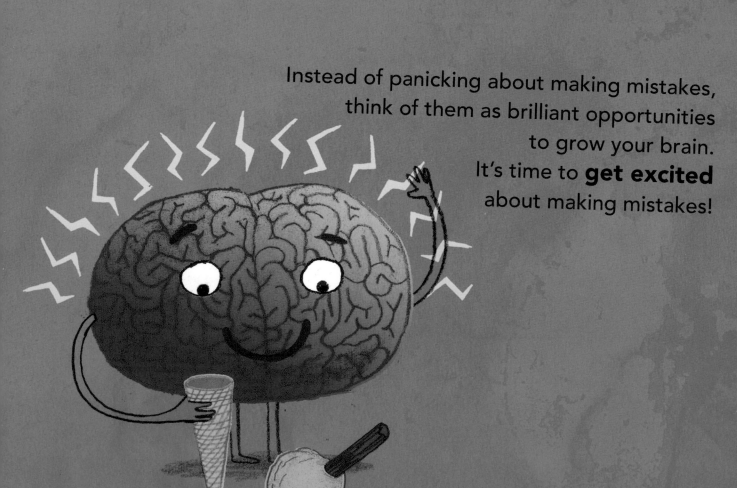

Look at the **snakes and ladders** board above – notice anything strange about it? There are ladders **AND** snakes in the same squares, because this is a special 'brain-growing' version.

Think of an **'easy win'** that the ladder could stand for – such as 'I find a subject easy without having to study'. Now think of the negative side that the snake could stand for – maybe 'I don't learn good study habits'.

Then try thinking of a **'big mistake'** that the snake could stand for – such as 'I get a lower mark than usual in my spelling test'. The ladder could stand for a great learning opportunity – perhaps 'I learn how to use flashcards to keep practising spellings I find tricky'.

The point of the activity isn't to win or lose the game. It shows how what feels negative in the short-term can be more positive in the long-term – and the other way around!

Tomorrow is another day

When things happen that make you feel really bad, it can sometimes seem like you'll never feel happy again. If you think **everything is ruined** and there's no going back to the way things were before, it is easy to start panicking.

But it's important to remember that everything changes and nothing lasts for ever. You've got through difficult things before, and gone from feeling bad to feeling happy again. There's no reason that this time is any different.

Rather than panicking, try thinking about what you can do to **fix things** or **feel happier**. What actions could you take to make tomorrow better than today?

Chris

A couple of months ago, I got **caught cheating** on a test in class and the teacher told me off in front of everyone. I was so embarrassed, I didn't want to go back to school the next day – my tummy hurt just thinking about it.

I told my dad about it, and we talked about why I felt like I had to cheat and what I could do now to make things better. I admitted that I hadn't really been paying attention in class, and then in the test I'd **panicked** when I didn't understand the questions.

I made two **'I'm Sorry'** cards to take in the next day – one for my teacher and one for my friend whose test I'd cheated from. I wrote a message in each card, explaining why I knew cheating was wrong and how I was going to do better in future.

My dad and I made a schedule to talk over school work together every evening, and it's really helping me to stay focused and keep putting in effort.

Remember: DON'T PANIC!

Read through these tips for a quick reminder of how best to **avoid panicking**!

Be a **future friend** to yourself. What can you do now to reduce your stress later on?

If you feel nervous about a new challenge, try telling yourself you're **excited about it** instead.

Start regular **Talk Time** sessions with a trusted adult, where you can talk to them about your worries.

If you don't believe in yourself, list times you've learned to do something before – **they're proof**!

If you're finding big changes difficult, plan with a trusted adult what you can do to feel **more positive**.

Find out, and practise, what makes you feel **calmer** when your brain starts to panic.

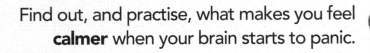

Make a **mind map** of your worries with a trusted adult, and look at each one in turn.

Remember that life **isn't a competition** – focus on your own brain-growing journey.

If you're worried about trying something new, **do some research** into it first.

Don't be afraid of **making mistakes** – learning from them helps your brain grow!

Instead of worrying that the worst will always happen, talk with a trusted adult and decide together what's **most likely** to happen.

If you think you've behaved badly, **don't panic** – think about how you can make it better tomorrow.

Notes for parents and teachers

The concept of a **'growth mindset'** was developed by psychologist Carol Dweck, and is used to describe a way in which effective learners view themselves as being on a constant journey to develop their intelligence. This is supported by studies showing how our brains continue to develop through our lives, rather than intelligence and ability being static.

Responding with a growth mindset means being eager to learn more, and seeing that making mistakes and getting feedback about how to improve are important parts of that journey.

A growth mindset is at one end of a continuum, and learners move between this and a 'fixed mindset' – which is based on the belief that you're either smart or you're not.

A fixed mindset is unhelpful because it can make learners feel they need to 'prove' rather than develop their intelligence. They may avoid challenges, not wanting to risk failing at anything, and this reluctance to make mistakes – and learn from them – can negatively affect the learning process.

Help children develop a growth mindset by:

- Giving specific positive feedback on their learning efforts, such as 'Well done, you've been practising …' rather than non-specific praise such as 'Good effort' or comments such as 'Clever girl/boy!' that can encourage fixed-mindset thinking.

- Sharing times when you have had to persevere with learning something new, and what helped you succeed.

- Encouraging them to keep a learning journal, where they can explore what they learn from new challenges and experiences.

- Helping them understand that they haven't done anything wrong if they do feel panicky, but it's not a nice feeling so that's why we work on developing positive habits to try to avoid it.

Glossary

fixed mindset thinking about your brain and intelligence as something fixed, and yourself and others as either smart or not

future friend being a 'future friend' to yourself means taking actions now to help you avoid panic in the future

growth mindset thinking about your brain as something that changes and grows, rather than something fixed that makes you either smart or not smart

neurons cells in your brain that pass information back and forth between one another

Talk Time time that you put aside every day to talk with a trusted adult about anything that is worrying you

Index

GROW YOUR MIND

978 1 4451 6860 9
978 1 4451 6861 6

978 1 4451 6923 1
978 1 4451 6924 8

978 1 4451 6925 5
978 1 4451 6926 2

978 1 4451 6927 9
978 1 4451 6928 6

978 1 4451 6930 9
978 1 4451 6929 3

978 1 4451 6931 6
978 1 4451 6932 3

978 1 4451 6933 0
978 1 4451 6934 7

978 1 4451 6935 4
978 1 4451 6936 1

Series contents

Boost Your Brain
- A brain-boosting mindset
- Sshhhhhhh...
- One thing at a time
- Think, rest, repeat
- Brain hugs
- Time out
- Take care of your body
- Brain dump
- Picture this
- Sum it up
- Make a mnemonic
- Study buddies
- Brainy book

Make Mistakes
- Mistakes and mindsets
- Feeling down
- Think again
- Types of mistake
- A new strategy
- A-ha!
- A healthy brain
- Time to shine
- Trying new things
- Don't give up
- Challenge o'clock
- My best mistake
- Famous failures

Think Positive
- A positive mindset
- Half-full or half-empty
- All or nothing
- Celebrate
- Thanks for everything
- Smile!
- Truly positive
- Let it go
- Feelings detective
- Seeing the future
- Positive people
- Doing good
- Be kind to yourself

Don't Panic
- A calm mindset
- Future friend
- Nervous or excited?
- Trust yourself
- Not a competition
- Panic button
- Reach out
- Everything changes
- Do your research
- What can I do?
- What could go wrong?
- If it does go 'wrong'
- Tomorrow is another day

Build Resilience
- A resilient mindset
- The power of 'yet'
- Effort thermometer
- Digging deeper
- Halfway there
- Try to fail
- Positive practice
- Stronger together
- Change for good
- Seeing the future
- Ups and downs
- Rest and recover
- Get creative

Work Smarter
- Mindsets at work
- Fighting fit
- Get chunking!
- Give it your all
- Activate your brain
- Just right
- Give your brain a chance
- Keep repeating
- Nobody's perfect
- How do they do it?
- Know yourself
- Work smart, play smart
- Be the teacher!

Face Your Fears
- Fear and mindsets
- What are you afraid of?
- Meet your fears
- You're not alone
- Being brave
- Little steps
- Big leaps
- Now isn't then
- Story time's over!
- Give it a minute
- See the other side
- Energy swap
- A year from today

Ask For Help
- Help and mindsets
- Everyone needs help
- Be brave
- Speaking up
- No stupid questions
- Who can help?
- Helping others
- Team power
- Taking feedback
- Sharing opinions
- Working through challenges
- Reaching out
- Helping yourself

FRANKLIN
WATTS